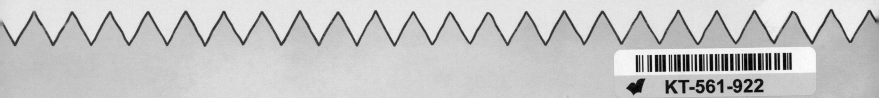

I Want to Be Tall!

Licensed by The Illuminated Film Company
Based on the LITTLE PRINCESS animation series © The Illuminated Film Company 2008.
Made under licence by Andersen Press Ltd., London
'I Want to Be Tall!' episode written by Laura Summers.
Producer Iain Harvey. Director Edward Foster.
© The Illuminated Film Company/Tony Ross 2008.
Design and layout © Andersen Press Ltd, 2008.
Printed and bound in China.

10 9 8 7 6 5 4 3 2

British Library Cataloguing in Publication Data available.

ISBN: 978 1 84270 768 5

I Want to Be Tall!

Tony Ross

Andersen Press · London

"Oh no!" cried the Little Princess. "Bouncy Thing is stuck!"
She had been having a lovely game outside with her space
hopper. She just hadn't meant to throw it quite so high.
The Little Princess stared up at the apple tree. "I'm not tall
enough to reach him."

"Dinnertime!" summoned the Maid.

"Oh goody!" grinned the Little Princess. "It's mashed potato and tomato sauce."

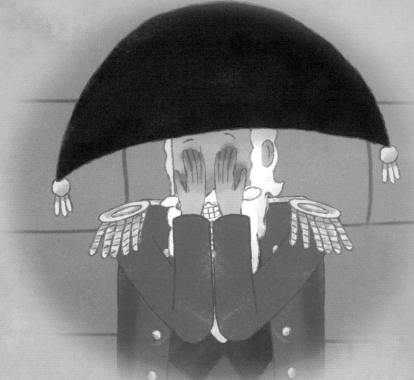

Inside, the Admiral, General and Prime Minister were playing hide and seek. "One, two, octopus, four…" muttered the Admiral. "Excuse me!" piped up the Little Princess.

"Sorry, Princess," said the Prime Minister. "Didn't spot you down there."
"You are a bit on the small side," tittered the General. The Little Princess scowled. "I need to get by!"

The Little Princess stood on her tiptoes in front of the fridge.
"I'm going to get the yummy ketchup," she decided.
On the third jump she managed to reach the handle and fling
open the door. Unfortunately the tomato sauce bottle was on
the top shelf.

"I need to be taller!" moaned the Little Princess.
"You'll be tall soon enough," said the King, cheerfully taking out
the ketchup.

"My *fantastique* dinner will make ze Little Princess grow big and tall," announced the Chef, filling her plate with bangers and mash.

"Ooh!" squealed the Little Princess. "More please!"

The Chef kept going…and going…and going until…

"There's none left for us!" cried the Queen.

The Little Princess got munching. "I'm going to grow very tall!"

By the time she'd climbed the stairs up to her bedroom, the Little Princess's tummy was feeling very full up.

"I ate too much dinner," she groaned. "But at least I'm taller now."

The Little Princess stood as straight as she could next to her height chart. To her dismay, she measured exactly the same as yesterday.

"That's not supposed to happen!"

"Your plant's taller than me!" grumbled the Little Princess when she spotted the Maid.

"But it did start off very tiny," said the Maid.

The Little Princess looked confused. "Why are you washing it?"

"I'm not!" laughed the Maid. "Plants need water to grow."

She began to explain, but the Little Princess had already disappeared.

"Whheeeee!"

The Little Princess leapt into her paddling pool with a splash.

"Growing tall is really good fun!" she giggled.

She pointed the hose up so it showered her in a bubbly

fountain of water, just like a giant watering can.

"That should do it," decided the Little Princess at last.

The Little Princess ran upstairs, dripping water all over the carpet. She marked her height on the chart with a green crayon. "Oh!" she wailed.

"I haven't grown at all!"

Nothing seemed to be working. "And my skin has gone all wrinkly," groaned the Little Princess.

She stared sadly out of the window. How was she ever going to rescue Bouncy Thing?

Over at the vegetable patch, the Gardener was measuring his prize pumpkins.

"What a whopper!" he chuckled. "Everything all right, Princess?"

The Little Princess frowned.

"Even your pumpkins are nearly as big as me."

"That's because I plant them in compost," replied the Gardener.

"Compost?"

The Gardener smiled confidently. "It never fails."

There was only one thing for it.

"It smells a bit pongy," spluttered the Little Princess, scrambling up the compost heap.

She stood amongst the soggy potato peelings and mouldy cabbage leaves for as long as she could bear it.

But when the Little Princess re-measured herself she hadn't grown a centimetre.
"Nothing!" she cried. "I want to be tall, tall, tall!"

The Little Princess was desperate. She sneakily lowered
the height chart, then drew a new purple line in crayon.
"I'm a great big Princess now!" she giggled.
The King wandered in. "Oh dear…"
The chart was quickly stuck back up in the right place.
"You're still my poppet, no matter how small you are,"
he explained.

"One day I will be tall," sighed the Little Princess. She gazed despairingly out of the window. Scruff and Puss were playing on the slide.

The Little Princess suddenly beamed. She had an idea.

"That's how I can be very, **very** tall!"

"I can reach Bouncy Thing now!" cried the Little Princess from the top of the slide. "And now that I am tall, I am not coming down ever! This is fun!"

Being tall came in very handy. The Little Princess was just the right height to help the Admiral win at hide and seek. She became the Chef's expert apple-picker.

She could even send her teddy,
Gilbert, on parachute adventures.

"Princess!" called the Maid. "Your auntie's just arrived with your
baby cousin."

The Little Princess waved hello.

"Can you just watch him for a minute for me?" asked the Maid.

The baby crawled over to Bouncy Thing, but he wasn't tall enough to climb on.

"I'll help you!"
shrieked the Little Princess.
"I'm tall enough!"
She was down the slide in a trice.
"You're much too small…

…but one day you'll grow nice and tall like me!"